She only wanted to help her friend, and now she was locked in a cave with no way out…

The man whined, "I do not know more. I was dead too, so how could I?"

Ellie wasn't satisfied. "Yes, you could. You saw them stabbing Orly, then you must have seen where they put him. You have to tell me."

The figure came closer. "Who are you? Why can I talk to you? I could bury you too."

Ellie took a breath. *I won't be afraid. He's not real anymore. He only wants to be as mean as before.* "I have special powers. You have to tell me, or else."

The baron cackled. "Or else, what? Even if I tell you, you can't escape. The entrance is blocked. Besides, I like company."

He's right, Ellie realized, *but first I have to know.* "Tell me!" she yelled at the top of her voice.

"In the barn, the barn, the barn! Now you know."

"Thank you. Now let me out." Ellie could only hope that the man had told the truth.

But he laughed. "You will have to tunnel yourself out."

Then the light and the figure disappeared, and the cave went dark and quiet.

During a visit to her grandmother's house, Ellie notices a stone arch in the garden that she has never seen before. Curious, she steps through it and meets a boy, Orly, who has been waiting for her. He tells her that he was killed two hundred years ago, and he needs Ellie's help to find his grave so he can go back to his village. Ellie knows that he's a ghost, and she's the only one who can see and talk to him. After hearing his story, she agrees to help, even though she has to go through many adventures. She's not even allowed to tell her grandmother about the details. Will Ellie succeed in convincing Grandma of her gift and giving the boy peace?

KUDOS for *Beyond the Stone Arch*

In *Beyond the Stone Arch* by Gisela Woldenga, Ellie discovers a secret stone arch in her grandmother's garden that leads to a forest near a village two centuries back in time. There Ellie meets Orly, a boy who was murdered two hundred years ago. He begs Ellie to find his grave so he can return to his village. In her quest to help Orly, Ellie has many harrowing adventures, putting her own life in jeopardy. Well written, exciting, and fast paced, this is a mid-grade story that young people should love. Well done for this talented author. ~ *Taylor Jones, The Review Team of Taylor Jones & Regan Murphy*

Beyond the Stone Arch by Gisela Woldenga is the story of eleven-year-old Ellie who is staying at her grandmother's house on vacation. In her grandmother's garden, Ellie finds an old stone arch with a gate leading into the past. She hears a flute playing, follows the music through the arch, and steps back two hundred years in time. Orly, the young boy playing the flute, tells Ellie that he has been waiting for her for two hundred years as she is the only one who can see him, so she is the only one who can help him. Orly needs Ellie to find his body. He was murdered and he doesn't know where they buried him. But even if Ellie can find out who killed Orly and where they buried him two hundred years ago, a lot can change in all that time, so will his body still even be there? *Beyond the Stone Arch* is intriguing, charming, and full of surprises. Woldenga's character development is superb and her plot solid. A great mid-grade story. ~ *Regan Murphy The Review Team of Taylor Jones & Regan Murphy*

ACKNOWLEDGMENTS

My many thanks to my Port Moody Writer's Group who have helped me through every chapter of this book.

Beyond the Stone Arch

Gisela Woldenga

A Black Opal Books Publication

GENRE: YA/MID GRADE/FANTASY/GHOST/PARANORMAL

BEYOND THE STONE ARCH
Copyright © 2019 by Gisela Woldenga
Cover Design by Jackson Cover Designs
All cover art copyright © 2019
All Rights Reserved
Print ISBN: 9781644370711

First Publication: JANUARY 2019

Published by Black Opal Books **http://www.blackopalbooks.com**

Beyond the Stone Arch

Chapter 1

Eleanor, don't go too far. Lunch is in half an hour." Grandmother's voice sounded serious.

Ellie stopped at the bottom step of the wooden stairs leading into the garden. "I'll be back. I have my watch."

If anyone called her Eleanor, she needed to listen. She checked her watch, a much-cherished present for her eleventh birthday. Eleven-thirty. Enough time to inspect the garden and maybe the grove of trees behind it.

Grandma loved her garden, her roses, beds of dahlias, pansies, azaleas, and some bushes that only bloomed in the spring. And a whole plot of vegetables.

She had told Ellie that each plant family needed different treatment. Ellie thought that sounded like they needed a doctor. Grandma just laughed.

"Different food and different amounts of water,"
she explained. "Like people."

By now Ellie's parents would be in Florida, visiting
some long-lost friends. Ellie would have liked to go
with them. But Mom said that they needed some time
alone. That was okay, Ellie liked it here. She could
roam around on her own, as long as she didn't upset
Grandma. Those were Mom's and Dad's orders. Ellie
looked up into the oak tree. She saw a branch low
enough to climb on, but not yet. She needed more time
for that.

A little farther on she saw a wooden fence at the
end of the garden. She noticed a break where another
part of the fence should have been. Instead there stood a
stone arch, overgrown with ivy. "Funny," Ellie thought.
"I've never seen that before." She looked at her watch.
Fifteen minutes. Time enough to investigate.

As she got closer to the archway, she heard someone playing a flute. Or was it a bird?

No, it sounded like a melody. Ellie brushed some of
the ivy away from the entrance and peeked through. At
first she only saw a grassy field with bushes. *Should I
step into it?* she thought. *This is probably just a left-
over stone door from way before.*

Again she heard the flute. "That music is so pretty," she said to herself. "Who's playing it?" Ellie took a few more steps onto the field and saw a boy sitting on a tree stump. He seemed to be absorbed in playing the flute and didn't look up.

I'll have to say something, Ellie thought. "You play really well," she called. "What are you doing here?"

The boy finished the part of the melody, stopped and looked at Ellie. "It sure took you a long time to get here," he said.

"What do you mean? I just arrived." Ellie found his comment a strange way of greeting. "What's your name? Mine is Ellie."

The boy brushed some leaves off his green jacket, got up and straightened his brown pants. "I call myself Orly because it's shorter than Orlando. I have been waiting for you, because nobody else wants to see me or talk to me."

Ellie was puzzled. "Don't you have parents or a grandma like me?" *He is taller than me*, she thought, *maybe older, too. And he has blond hair*.

Orly sat down again. "I used to—a long time ago."

"So, are you an orphan? Where do you live?"

Orly picked up his flute. "You ask too many questions. You have to come back. Go, your grandma is waiting." With that, he started playing again, the same sweet melody as before.

Ellie looked at her watch. Only five minutes to go. "Okay, I'll see you a bit later." Even if he wasn't the friendliest boy she had ever met, he had piqued her interest. She needed to know more about Orly and his flute.

She rushed back through the garden and up the steps into the kitchen. Grandma smiled. "Good girl, you're on time. Put some glasses on the table."

Ellie couldn't wait to tell her about her discovery. "There is this stone arch at the end of your garden. I went through and met a boy called Orly. He plays the flute and is an orphan." She stopped to catch her breath.

Grandma sliced some bread. "What arch are you talking about? I've never seen a stone arch."

"But you must have. It's right at the end by the wooden fence." How could she not, Ellie thought. Grandma has lived here all her life.

But Grandmashook her head. "You must have been dreaming. You used to see elves in the garden when you were little, remember?"

Ellie covered her slice of bread with butter. "Yeah, I know. But today I didn't see any, only the boy. He plays the flute really well. And I have to go again later to see him. He's all alone."

Grandma looked at her. "After lunch you have to show me this arch. I wonder if you got too much sun."

Ellie was happy. She couldn't wait to see the look

of surprise on Grandma's face at the sight of the arch-way and the sound of Orly's flute.

Chapter 2

Ellie knew she had to dry the lunch dishes and put them away. Grandma had her rules. Ellie didn't mind, only today everything took too long. Finally, Grandma had cleaned the kitchen sink and hung up the towel.

"Now show me what you saw," she said.

Ellie skipped ahead of her down the steps. "You'll be surprised."

When they reached the end of the garden she pointed at the wooden fence. "Can you see it, Grandma? There it is, there—" She stopped. No arch. "But it was right here, I went through it." Ellie couldn't move. How could that be?

Grandma walked toward the fence and looked over. "Where was the boy? It's all meadow out there."

Ellie felt like crying. "I wasn't lying, the arch stood here, and Orly played the flute."

Grandma put her hand on Ellie's shoulder. "I believe you. As I said, you used to see elves, and I didn't. You are a special girl. But think first: Did you read a story about something like this? Maybe you pictured it in your mind."

Ellie shook her head. "No, never. My last book was all about a girl, not a boy and no stone arches."

Grandma walked back to the house. "Let's have some ice cream. Then you can decide what to do. As long as you don't disappear, too."

Ellie didn't know what to think. Why was the arch there, and an hour later it wasn't? Why didn't she hear the flute? She had to admit it had been weird. But she had promised to go back and see Orly and that's exactly what she was going to do. She had to find out more.

The ice cream calmed her down a bit. Could it be that Orly didn't want to meet Grandma? But why not? She was kind and had even said that Ellie was special. *And why didn't I notice the arch on an earlier visit?* Ellie wondered. When Grandma laid down for a nap, Ellie took her small camera and went out into the garden. Maybe if she took a picture of the stone door and the boy, she would have proof.

Her heart pounded as she walked through the garden. Would Orly be back again? Just a few steps away from the wooden fence she heard the flute. Yes! She hadn't been dreaming. There stood the arch with ivy hanging all over it. Ellie pulled out her camera and took a picture. Just to be safe, she clicked off another one. Then she stepped through the door. Orly sat by the big tree again playing the tune she liked so much. He stopped.

"So, you did come back," he said and stood up.

Ellie walked over. "Of course, I promised. I came here earlier to show Grandma, but you and the arch weren't here. Why did you do that?"

"This isn't for her to see, it's for you. I want to show you something." Orly stuck the flute into his pant pocket and motioned to Ellie.

She got excited. "Something nice or weird?"`

Orly waved her over. "You have to come with me into the trees. What you'll see is special and important. Don't be noisy or cry out. Be quiet, okay?"

"I promise. But if it's scary, I might—"

Orly shook his head. "It's not scary, just different."

Ellie felt pangs of doubt. Should she go? Would she be able to come back here? She didn't say anything. Orly shouldn't think that she was a scaredy-cat. She followed him through the trees but kept looking back at the big oak tree. That would be the marker to return to.

After walking for a while, Orly stopped and pointed to an opening between the trees. As Ellie looked, it got wider and turned into a dirt road with small houses on both sides. People walked around and a horse-drawn cart bumped along. If Orly hadn't cautioned her not to shout, she would have. *They need new clothes*, she thought. *They look so shabby. What kind of place is this?*

"Where are we?" she whispered.

"In my village," Orly answered. "I used to live here."

Ellie stopped. "But this looks old, like some pictures in my history book. How can you be here now? Is this magic? What will these people think of us?"

Orly put his finger to his lips. "They can't see us," he whispered. "*Here* we are ghosts, in *your* world, they are. They might still hear us." He pointed to an old lady with a blue shawl covering her head. "She might. She's a seer and helps sick people."

"Is she a witch?"

Orly shook his head. "We don't call her that. She's a good person with a special gift." Slowly he walked on.

Ellie was afraid that she might bump into some of the villagers, but they seemed to go about their business without noticing her. She had to swallow a creepy feeling about all this. She looked at Orly. He stood quietly and watched. Somehow she knew she could trust him. *It has to be important to him to bring me here*, she thought. *But I have so many questions. He will have to do a lot of explaining.*

Chapter 3

Orly walked farther down the dusty road, toward what looked like a huge oven. "I used to carry loads of wood for it and helped to mix flour for baking bread."

"In there?" Ellie pointed to the oven. "How did you get the bread out?"

Orly smiled. "With a long wooden plank. Watch."

Two men came out of the house and opened the oven door. They shoved a long-handled piece of wood into it and retrieved four round loaves of bread. A beautiful aroma drifted toward Ellie.

"That smells so good," she whispered.

After taking more loaves out of the oven, the bakers replaced them with a new load of unbaked ones.

"Everyone in the village needs bread in the morning," Orly said. "They have to bake quite a lot." Then he turned.

A faint voice called out, "Orlando."

"She has seen us."

Ellie turned around too. The old lady with the blue shawl stood close and stared at them.

Orly sighed. "Martha. I hoped you would not see us."

Martha's voice sounded barely above a whisper. "You have come back."

"No, not yet. I will need more help."

Martha pointed at Ellie. "Who is she?"

Orly put his hand on Ellie's arm. "She might be able to help me."

A strange feeling went through Ellie. She hadn't expected him to have such a solid touch. After all, wasn't Orly like the other people here—a ghost? Or was all of this magic?

The old lady stared at Ellie again.

She looks right through me, Ellie thought, *like Mom when I have done something wrong.*

Then Martha turned to Orly. "Be careful. Keep her safe."

With that, she shuffled away.

Orly sighed again. "She notices more than anyone else." He waved his hand around. "Maybe you can, too, or else you wouldn't see this."

"Because you brought me here. Otherwise I wouldn't have." She looked up at him. "Why did you? Why aren't you with these people?"

"I'll tell you more about that later. Let's go back."

Ellie heaved a sigh of relief. She had to think about this. If Orly didn't conjure up the village with magic, how did it happen? Martha and the other villagers appeared to be so real and part of Orly's life. So, why wasn't he in the village too?

He marched ahead fast, and Ellie, deep in thought, stumbled after him. At one point, she looked back, but the village was gone. Then she saw something glitter on the ground. She bent down and brushed off some leaves. The object was round and golden like a medal, smooth with something engraved on the surface. "Look what I found," she called.

Orly stopped and waited. His eyes got big when he looked at the golden piece in Ellie's hand. "This was mine." His voice quivered. He turned the medal over and polished the top with his jacket sleeve. "It has an oak leaf etched on it." He looked at Ellie. "This is a good omen. Here, you have it. You might need it."

"But it's yours," Ellie protested. "I can't keep it."

"You'll have to. I'll tell you my story and hope that

you'll help me. This will be your good-luck charm."

Ellie turned the golden disc around in her hand.
"It's beautiful. Who gave it to you?"

Orly sat down on his tree stump. "My grandfather
before he died. And then—" He stopped and took a
breath. "—someone stole it."

She still wasn't sure of what to do with it. "What
use would I have for it?"

Orly took out his flute. "It's a long story. I'll tell
you tomorrow. Don't say anything to your grandmother
about this, please. Now you have to go home." Without
waiting for Ellie's reply, he started to play.

"Okay." She knew that he wouldn't talk any more,
not when he played his flute.

She turned and went back through the arch. As she
walked along the flowerbeds she could still hear the
melody drifting from the meadow. She sat down on the
garden bench. All that she had seen—the village, Martha, and Orly in the middle of it—flipped around in her
mind like a kaleidoscope. Had it been real or some sort
of trick? She looked at the golden medal again. This at
least was real. She had to hide it in her pants pocket
since Grandma wasn't allowed to see it. To keep quiet
about it was going to be hard. For the answers to the
many questions, Ellie needed to wait until tomorrow.
She sighed. It would be a long night.

Chapter 4

The next morning, Ellie couldn't wait until breakfast was over. Orly was probably already looking for her. But Grandma had other plans.

"I need to buy groceries this morning," she said. "I want you to come with me."

Ellie's happy mood fell like a deflated balloon. "But I need to meet Orly. Can't I stay here?"

Grandma shook her head. "I'm responsible for you and don't want you to be alone in the house."

Ellie tried again. "I'm eleven years old, not a little kid. What could happen to me?"

Grandma gave her a sharp look. "You can see Orly in the afternoon." Then she smiled. "I'll take you for lunch, okay?"

"Can I at least leave him a note?"

Grandma grabbed her handbag. "Can he read?"

What a question, Ellie thought. But it occurred to her that she didn't remember seeing a school in the village. Maybe he never learned to read? She sighed. "Can we buy some ice cream bars?"

Grandma chuckled, locked the door, and they walked down to the car.

During the drive to the grocery store, Ellie could not help thinking about Orly waiting for her. She almost heard him play his flute. Grandma looked at her.

"Orly will wait. Don't worry."

"I just don't want him to think that I have broken my promise."

Grandma patted her hand. "He knows."

"How do you know?" Ellie asked.

Grandma steered into a parking spot. "I've lived for a long time. I think I know about boys like Orly."

Ellie still didn't quite understand. Yes, Grandma was old, but she couldn't see Orly. How would she know about him?

At least shopping was done quickly. Grandma knew what she wanted and where to find it.

Sitting in the restaurant, Ellie thought, *Mom never*

lets me order a hamburger and fries but Grandma doesn't mind.

"Just this once," she'd said.

But when Grandma started to chit-chat with the waitress, Ellie got antsy. *Let's go*, she thought. *Orly is waiting.*

Grandma finally said, "Let's be on our way," and Ellie heaved a sigh of relief.

Back at home, Ellie helped carry the groceries into the kitchen. "Can I go now?" she asked.

Grandma waved her away. "Go. Run."

Ellie jogged through the garden and stood still. No arch and no sound of the flute. A wave of panic shot through her. "I knew it!" she wailed. "He got tired of waiting. Orly, where are you?" Then the arch appeared. Ellie raced toward it. "Please, don't play tricks on me."

Orly sat on the tree stump. "What took you so long?"

"Grandma needed groceries. I'm sorry." *He looks sad*, Ellie thought. Dad had a word for it: pensive. "Are you okay?" she asked.

Orly nodded. "It's just hard to tell my story, because I don't have an answer."

Ellie sat on the grass beside him. "But I'm curious. Tell me anyway."

He pulled his knees up and wrapped his arms around them. "There used to be a big mansion on the grounds where your grandma's house stands. The stone arch marked the end of the property. A man lived there with his family. We called him *the baron*. He looked after our village, but he wasn't a nice man. He didn't treat his servants well. I had to bring him vegetables, bread, and, sometimes, chickens. One day, close to Christmas, the snow was deep, and it took me longer to get there. I had a big turkey in a sack for him. When I got there, the baron was mad that I was late. He took the turkey and said, 'It is not big enough. You are cheating me.' I wasn't, I only delivered it. When I asked for the money he owed for it, he really got angry. He pushed me into the snow and kicked me. I called out that I was sorry, that it wasn't my fault. He picked something up from the ground and came at me. I cannot remember anything else." Orly stopped. He rocked back and forth.

Ellie was shocked. "Oh, no! What a beast. Did he hurt you?"

Orly shrugged. "The people in the village say that I never came back, that I had disappeared. They searched for me and asked everyone, but nobody could tell them anything. I want you to find me."

Ellie stared at him. "What do you mean? Find you? You're here. Where else can you be?"

He shook his head. "You don't understand. I need to find the rest of me, wherever I am."

"You mean the baron killed you and—and—" She

closed her eyes. She had a hard time thinking clearly. His story was too sad and unbelievable. She took the medal out of her pants pocket. She needed something to hold onto.

After a long time, Orly said, "I'm glad you found my medal. I had it in my jacket pocket at that time. When I woke up here, it was gone. Maybe the baron was the one who stole it."

"Why didn't you wake up in the village? Why here? And why do you play the flute?" Ellie blurted the questions out as fast as she could. She didn't want Orly to tell her to go home.

He shrugged. "I guess I had to be near the baron's house. Maybe I needed to wait for you. And I used to take care of sheep in the fields. Out of boredom, I played the flute."

Ellie felt defeated. How could she possibly find the real Orly? Or the rest of him, as he had said. What would she find?

As if reading her mind, Orly said, "You have to go back into the village, this time without me. Find Martha, she might help you."

"Without you?" Panic rose inside her. "I won't find the village. I'm scared thinking about it."

Orly grabbed his flute. "If you don't want to try, I'll never get back to the village. And you don't need to come back here."

She was shocked. "No, No! How can you think that? I'll help. But let me think about it. My head feels like mush. I'm only eleven years old."

Orly smiled again. "I knew you would. You have the gift to do it. Go home now." This time, he put the flute to his mouth and played.

Again, Ellie sat down on the garden bench. What did he mean by '*You have the gift?*' What gift? Was that what Grandma meant by being *special?* Because Grandma couldn't see what Ellie could? She held her head in her hands. *How can I do this?* Then she sat up straight. No matter what Orly had said, Ellie had to ask Grandma some questions.

Chapter 5

A delicious smell of meat roasting met Ellie when she walked up the wooden steps. "I'm home!" she called and went into the bathroom to wash her hands. She looked into the mirror and brushed her dark, unruly hair back. *How can I possibly do what Orly wants?* she thought. *I need to ask Grandma about this house. Maybe she knows something about the old mansion.*

She heard Grandma calling, "Dinner is ready."

While they were eating, Grandma asked, "You are so quiet. Is something on your mind?"

Ellie nodded. "When did you build this house, Grandma?"

"I didn't, my great-great-grandfather did."

Ellie stopped between bites of chicken. "How come it doesn't look old?"

Grandma put down her fork. "It started out smaller and each next owner added more onto it. Grandpa and I renovated quite a bit. It's still quite solid. It'll last as long as I live."

Ellie mashed her potatoes with gravy. "You'll live for a long time, Grandma. But—" *Here goes.* "Did you know there was a mansion here before with a mean baron?"

Grandma chuckled. "Oh, my. Orly seems to know a lot about this area. I only heard about an old house that was falling apart before this one was built. There were stories about a cruel man who threw his servants out into the snow to let them freeze to death. One never knows how much of it is true. They're just stories."

"No, they are not." Ellie bit her lip. Should she say more? But she had to. "He killed Orly."

Grandma looked at her for a long time. Ellie got worried. *Why doesn't she answer?* Then Grandma wiped her hands on her napkin and said, "Be careful what you believe, Ellie. If Orly wants you to do something, think about it carefully. You're just starting to find out things about yourself. As I said before, you're in my care now."

How much does Grandma really know? Ellie wondered. "I promise not to upset you. I'll be careful. But why did you say that I was special? Because I'm your granddaughter?"

Grandma stacked the dishes. "Of course. But also because you see more of our world than I can. I had a great-great-aunt who apparently could."

Seeing things, Ellie thought, *like I see Orly and the village. Good thing I didn't tell Grandma about the forest.* "Well, so I'm different," she said. "I don't feel different. Thanks for supper. It was delicious."

Grandma smiled. "Your turn to do the dishes."

ᴇᴑᴇᴑ

Ellie lay awake for a long time that night. Constant *what-ifs* were popping into her mind. What if she couldn't find the village or her way home? What if Martha didn't like her? What if the villagers saw her this time? And Orly wasn't with her to help. Grandma could be right: how much of all this was real? *But Orly is*, she thought. *He is so sad. He wants to go back to his village and can't until his real body has been found. I wish I could find it without going back into the village. But where could it be after how long? Way over a hundred years for sure. His medal is real.* Ellie got out of bed and looked into her pants pocket. There it was, all shiny. It fitted into the palm of her hand. She stroked it gently. *What if it has magical powers?*

She walked over to the window. She could see the stars and a sliver of the moon. Everything was so quiet. *Maybe if I pray I'll get help*, she thought. "If you have time to listen to me, dear God, please, help me to help Orly. He needs to go home. I hope you have punished the baron, but, please help."

She felt a bit better after that and crawled back into bed. Then she dreamed of Martha staring at her again.

ⲉⲟⲉⲟ

After breakfast the next morning Ellie noticed that Grandma looked at her again for a long time. It made her feel uncomfortable. When she had finished her pancakes, Grandma said, "I don't want to keep you from seeing Orly, Ellie. But you have to promise not to go running off to where you can't hear me calling you. I also have some friends coming over this afternoon for tea. I would like you to come and say hello."

I guess, I'll have to, Ellie thought. *After all, Grandma is so understanding.* "Okay, I'll try and be here. See you at lunchtime." With that, she scooted out the door and down the steps. Maybe Orly had figured out a way to find his body without her going into the village.

The arch stood in its place but Orly was not there. Ellie could hear his flute but from where? She walked farther down the meadow and finally saw him sitting on a rock between two bushes. "Why are you here?" she asked. "I got worried."

Orly got up. "I did play the flute so you could hear me." He waved his hand around. "This was different the last time, more fields and cows. I was looking for something, but it's not here anymore."

"What is it?"

Orly shrugged. "Just something I remember."

Ellie held her breath. "Something where you could be?"

He walked toward his former place by the trees. "I just don't know."

"Then we have to dig there. I'll get a spade." Ellie was ready to run.

Orly held her back. "No, you would dig forever. Where would you start? You have to go to the village."

"But I can't, not today. I promised Grandma to be there for lunch and say hello to her friends at tea time." She paced around. *Why today?*

He looked sad again. "Oh, yes, the baron had lunches and teas. But we didn't have enough food."

He looked up. Ellie saw a shadow creeping over his face. Was there something he hadn't told her? Why couldn't she see more? She sighed. "I don't know what to do now. I can't upset Grandma, and I don't want to upset you either. Why did you pick me?"

"Because you're connected to this place, and you're like Martha, at least a bit."

Ellie sat down on the grass. "Like Martha? No way. She looked right through me. I'm scared of her."

Orly shook his head. "She wouldn't hurt you. But I think she knows more than I do about what happened to me."

Ellie got up. She had made up her mind. "I can't do anything today. How about tomorrow?" Her head started to ache. She needed to think about this whole Martha-thing again. How much could she know about Orly's death? It all sounded more and more puzzling. And as Grandma had said, "Think about it carefully." One more day couldn't possibly make that much of a difference, could it?

Chapter 6

Ellie didn't look back when she walked through the arch. She didn't know why she felt angry. Yes, she was going to help him, but the way he talked sometimes bothered her. She knew his death made him sad. But there seemed to be something else, and he hadn't told her what. Shouldn't she know everything before she went back to the village? *I'll have to do something else now to feel bette*r. Maybe if she would write her experiences into her diary, she wouldn't feel angry any more. *As if anyone would believe that story*, she thought.

After lunch, she went into her room and dug her diary out of her suitcase. At first, she didn't know how to

start. But after a few tries it came easier. What difference did it make if her grammar wasn't correct? Ellie
was the only one who would read it, certainly not her
teacher.

Ellie didn't know how long she had been writing
when voices drifted from the front door up to her room.
Grandma's visitors. Somehow Ellie felt easier, like she
had put her thoughts into order. *Tomorrow I'm going to
find the village.*

Three ladies sat around the kitchen table, all like
Grandma: white-haired and smiling. After Ellie shook
their hands Grandma said, "Sit down and have tea with
us. I baked a special cake."

Do I have to? Ellie thought. *I don't know what to
talk to them about.* But she knew she had to be polite.
The ladies asked the usual questions: "How old are
you? Where do you live? Do you like school? Do you
have hobbies?"

She almost giggled at that question. *What if I tell
them that I see things they can't? No, better not.*

Ellie finished her tea and cake and asked to be ex-
cused. She decided to finally climb up that branch into
the oak tree. After a few missteps, she reached a secure
place and looked around. No stone arch and no Orly.

*He knows I'm coming tomorrow. What is he doing
in the meantime? Where is he going?* Ellie dangled her

legs. *If I think about it, it'll just make me squirmy inside.*

From up there she could see a few of the neighbors' houses. *What would it have looked like two-hundred years ago?* she thought. *Except for the baron's mansion, could there have been more small villages around?* It was so quiet up here, she let her mind wander. She imagined the snowy day when Orly had delivered the turkey. She pictured the baron's big house. What would he have looked like? He was mean, so he was probably big and even fat. And Orly looked so small and skinny. But someone else seemed to be around. Maybe servants.

Voices woke Ellie out of her daydream. She shook her head. *I was almost there with Orly,* she thought. She looked down. Grandma and her guests were walking around in the garden. Those were the voices Ellie had heard. But now she had to get down. Strong winds had come up and were shaking the branches. *The leaves are whispering to me*, she thought. *The tree probably saw what happened to Orly. It's so old.* Ellie sighed. Maybe tonight I dream about something that could help me.

The next morning, Ellie only remembered her dreams flowing by like a sped-up movie. She worried about how to tell Grandma that she might not be back by lunch. Ellie didn't know how long she would be in the village. What if Martha wanted to talk to her?

After stirring her cereal and spooning some blue-berries over it, she tried. "Grandma, would it be okay if I skipped lunch today? Orly wants to show me some things."

Grandma sipped her tea. "What things?"

Ellie hesitated. "Well, I don't know exactly yet. But we're going for a walk, and it might be a long one."

Grandma wrinkled her brow. "I can only hope that you're smart enough to keep your mind open to any-thing that sounds or looks dangerous, Eleonore. If Orly was killed around here, the mystery will not be far."

But I need the village to find out, Ellie thought. "Grandma, do you believe in ghosts?"

Grandma refilled her teacup. "I have not seen any, but maybe there are souls that cannot find any rest. Look at Orly."

Ellie nodded. *Yes, Orly is a ghost, after all.* "But I have never seen any other ones."

"You probably will, my child, you will. Just do not ask for it." Grandma got up and collected the dishes. "Try to be back as soon as you can, promise?"

"Oh, yes, I will. Cross my heart. Thank you." *Grandma is the best in the world*, Ellie thought.

Outside, the wind was still blowing and pushing the clouds by fast. "Please, don't rain," Ellie called, "at least not today." She jogged through the garden and the arch. Orly was playing his flute again. This time, the melody sounded different, sort of jumpy, dancey. He didn't stop until she stood in front of him.

"Good morning. What do I have to do now?" Ellie asked.

Orly got up. "I'll walk with you to the beginning of the forest," he said. "Then you'll have to go on alone."

"Why?" Ellie still hoped to hear a proper reason for it.

"Because I don't know how I died, and you have to find out."

Ellie was puzzled. "But you were killed, you know that."

Orly shrugged. "I feel something is missing. You have to look for it."

"I don't know what I'm looking for. Are you sure I'll be okay in there? I mean—" She stopped. "I'm a bit scared, you know."

Orly put his hand on her shoulder. "Please, go. Do you have my medal? Martha will see you and help you."

Ellie swallowed. A promise is a promise. "All right, I'll try."

Together they walked to the big oak tree. Orly stopped. Ellie looked at him once more and stepped into the shadow of the forest.

Chapter 7

Ellie's heart pounded. "Please, let me find the village," she whispered.

She didn't know if anyone would hear her plea, but she needed to ask anyway. All she heard was the rustling of the leaves and a few squirrels scurrying up and down trees. *How deep into the forest did we go?* She checked at her watch. Only five minutes? Maybe time stood still in here. Ellie stopped and took a breath. *Okay, keep going. I can do this.*

She kept walking. The path got wider and finally it opened up into a round, empty space. Ellie waited. Where was the village? She tried to think really hard. *Come on, I need the village. Come on.*

Little by little, she saw houses appear, the dusty street, and even the horse and wooden wagon rumbling through it. Ellie tried to swallow down the butterflies in her stomach. She hoped that the people wouldn't see her.

Carefully, she stepped forward. Children played and ran around her. Ellie stayed out of their way. But they didn't pay attention to her. *Where am I supposed to go now? Where do I start?* She walked on.

Soon the big ovens came into view again. And again the smell of fresh-baked bread wafted toward her. The last time Orly had stopped here, but the street seemed to go on now. Ellie followed it and came to a small church made out of gray stone. At home, the churches were much bigger, with tall steeples. This one looked no bigger than a normal house. In the front, on top of the roof, stood what seemed to her like two chimneys.

As Ellie looked closer, she noticed two narrow windows in them with a bell in each one. A bell tower. What would the church look like inside?

Ellie walked the narrow path toward the entrance. She noticed gravestones on the right side of the church. *Are there names on them?* She bent down and read *Mary, 1786.* That was all she could make out. *Boy, 1786? Wow, that's old.* A sound came from the church, and the door opened. An old man came out clad in a long black coat. The pastor? He walked right past Ellie but didn't see her.

I'll have a peek inside, she decided.

The brown door creaked when she opened it. She stepped into a small place with another door at the end. Its blue color had flaked off in places, and the wooden door knob was shiny. Carefully, Ellie turned it. Inside, she waited for a moment to get used to the dim light before she moved forward. The floor crackled under her feet. Benches and chairs stood lined-up on each side of the aisle. Three narrow windows on both side of the two walls shed a pale light into the room. Two of them had stained glass with roses in them. The cross with Jesus hung on the far wall over a small altar. *So simple*, Ellie thought. *Did Orly attend services here?* She heard a rustling in one of the front benches. A soft voice called.

"Come in, dear, come in."

Ellie froze. She wanted to run but couldn't. Again she heard the voice.

"Don't be frightened. I was waiting for you."

Martha? Could that be her? She sounded so much stronger than last time. Slowly, Ellie walked to the front. On the first bench, the old lady with the blue shawl sat and looked up at her. Again, Ellie had the feeling that Martha stared right through her. But this time it did not bother her.

Martha pointed to the seat beside her. "Sit down. I cannot stay long. I have to speak to you. You have to listen. You are brave and kind. But you still have to let go of fear of whatever you meet and see."

Ellie sat down. "That's hard. But how can you even talk to me after such a long time?"

Martha smiled a little. "I am a seer, as you are now. No magic."

"What should I do now? I don't know where to start."

Martha adjusted her shawl. "You have to find the baron."

Ellie's mouth fell open. Did she hear that right? "The baron? Oh, no. He's mean and will kill me too."

Martha shook her head. "No, he cannot. He was a bad man, but he did not kill Orlando."

Ellie didn't know what to say. If not the baron, then who? "But Orly remembered the baron hitting him with something."

"He did not kill him. Orlando is lost because he feels something is not right. Only the baron knows. I saw things but not clearly. You have to find out. Orlando is my sister's boy." Martha's voice got softer and fainter.

Ellie got panicky again. "Don't go, Martha! Where do I find the baron? And what if he doesn't see me?"

Martha rose from her seat. "Go to the end of the village and use your mind," she whispered. "He only sees you if you want him to."

Quickly, Ellie asked, "How do I use my mind?"

But Martha had already moved to the church door and was gone.

Ellie sat very still on the bench. *How can I do this?* she asked herself again. *It's getting so complicated. The last person I want to meet is the baron. Even ghosts can hurt people if they're angry. How can I just make him appear? But that's what Martha had said, "Use your mind."*

Ellie straightened up. *I made the village appear a while ago by thinking hard. I'll just have to try and do the same with the baron and not be scared.* That was what Martha had told her, too. Ellie gave a big quivery sigh. *But I am scared. Why did I have to meet Orly? Right, because I could see him.*

Chapter 8

Ellie was on her way to the church door when it opened and the man in the black coat walked in. Ellie scooted to the side. *Please, don't see me*, she thought. *He must be the pastor or Vicar.*

He walked to the back of the church and searched for something under the altar. He picked up what looked like the bible and began reading. Ellie tip-toed out of the door. *Maybe he's preparing for a sermon.* Outside, she saw people coming up the walk. Yes, he was going to preach. *Should I listen? But I don't have time. Grandma is probably waiting already.*

Ellie continued up the main road. How far away was the end of the village that Martha had talked about?

And where would the baron be? A few steps farther, two dogs ran toward her. They stopped and looked at her. One started to growl, and the hair on its neck stood up. She shivered. *They can see me. I'll have to talk to them.* Quietly she said, "Shh, don't bite. I won't hurt you, I love dogs. You're good boys, aren't you?" *Can they understand me? Can I walk away?* "Don't see me, just go on," she whispered.

With another look at her, the dogs trotted down the road. Ellie took a big breath. She had heard that animals could see things that people were not able to. What about wild animals? Her heart started pounding again.

"Use your mind," Martha had said.

I'll have to try hard. Right now I have to find the end of the village.

People were still walking around her. Flickering lights came on in some of the houses. *Oh, no, is it that late? Grandma will be so upset.* Ellie walked faster. She could see a stand of trees not far away. Was that the end of the village? She started jogging. Close to the trees, she came to a sharp drop-off. Everything around her was draped in a strange fog.

I'll have to climb down, she thought. *There are rocks I can step on.* She got a foothold on the first rock then the second. But the third started to slip, and Ellie found herself sliding the rest of the way into a small gully.

Ellie sat there for a few minutes. Her right hand had a few scratches, but it didn't hurt too much. She stood and dusted herself off. *What a mess, but it's only sand. Now what?* Looking around, she noticed a big hole in the side of the rock. A cave? Would the baron be inside? Butterflies invaded her stomach again.

Cautiously, Ellie stepped closer. She brushed away some vines hanging over the entrance. *Good thing they're not spider webs. Another doorway.* It was just big enough for her to squeeze through. Inside, she stopped and listened. No sounds except for a faint drip-drip of water somewhere. *It's chilly in here and spooky. How far in does it go? I should have brought a flashlight. But how did I know I would end up in a cave?* After a few more steps, Ellie saw a faint light, more like something shimmering in the background. Was that where the baron lived?

Ellie called, "Is anyone there?"

No answer.

She shook her head. *Why would a dead baron be in a cave? He should be in a cemetery.* Then she heard a sound. With a loud bang and rattle, rocks clattered down into the entrance behind her and filled it up. Ellie yelled, "Nooo! I need to get out again. I don't want to be stuck in here!"

For the first time, she was *really* scared. Her breath came in short gasps. She willed herself to calm down.

"Don't be afraid," Martha had said. "Use your mind." *Okay, first I'll go toward the funny light out there. It has to lead to somewhere.* Then she remembered Orly's medal. Yes, it still sat safely in her pants pocket. She had to make sure not to lose it.

With her left hand, she felt along the cave's cold stone wall and walked slowly ahead. The light ahead flickered. Ellie thought she saw movements too. But the closer she thought she got to it, the farther it shrank away. *Is the baron tricking me?* Then she got angry. *What did Dad used to say?*

"I won't stand for it!" she called it out and listened. A low growl was her answer. Who or what was really hiding there?

Finally Ellie heard a low voice. "What are you doing here, disturbing my peace? What do you want?'"

Ellie crept closer to the flickering lights. "If you're the baron, I want to know why you killed Orly."

Another growl. Then, "That little village rat, it was all his fault. His fault that I'm dead, but good that he's dead too."

Ellie stomped her feet. "He's not a rat. He was a boy doing a job for you. You killed him. Where did you bury him?"

There came a high piercing howl. "No, no, no! I did not. I could not!"

"But you clobbered him and he fell into the snow."

After another howl, the baron yelled, "I did not kill him, I saw him move. But I got stabbed and ended up in here." He groaned again.

How much can I believe him? Ellie wondered. "Then how come Orly died, and where's his body?" She had crept closer to the light and noticed an outline of a body moving back and forth. "Tell me what happened," she called.

After a pause, the baron grumbled, "Two servants stabbed me. They hated me. Then they stabbed the boy because he woke up and saw them."

Ellie nodded, feeling like she was finally getting closer to the truth. "Where did they put him? Nobody could find him."

The man whined, "I do not know more. I was dead too, so how could I?"

Ellie wasn't satisfied. "Yes, you could. You saw them stabbing Orly, then you must have seen where they put him. You have to tell me."

The figure came closer. "Who are you? Why can I talk to you? I could bury you too."

Ellie took a breath. *I won't be afraid. He's not real anymore. He only wants to be as mean as before.* "I have special powers. You have to tell me, or else."

The baron cackled. "Or else, what? Even if I tell you, you can't escape. The entrance is blocked. Besides, I like company."

He's right, Ellie realized, *but first I have to know.* "Tell me!" she yelled at the top of her voice.

"In the barn, the barn, the barn! Now you know."

"Thank you. Now let me out." Ellie could only hope that the man had told the truth.

But he laughed. "You will have to tunnel yourself out."

Then the light and the figure disappeared, and the cave went dark and quiet.

Chapter 9

Ellie braced herself against the cold cave wall. She shivered. In the sudden darkness she didn't dare to move. She yelled, "Bring back the light. I can't see anything."

There was no answer.

What was she going to do now? She saw some tiny pin points of light through the cracks between the fallen rocks at the entrance. She focused on them and moved forward.

"Orly, help me out of here," she called. She felt something warm in her pants pocket. *The medal, Orly's good-luck charm.* But it was only a piece of metal. Ellie took it out and gently rubbed the smooth surface. It got warmer and started to glow. Had it come alive? With her back touching the wall, Ellie slid toward the entrance. "Can you help me?" she whispered.

The glow grew stronger. Ellie didn't know why, but she pointed it at the rocks and held her breath. A light beam shot out of the disc and made a hole in between the rocks. *That was amazing! Where did that power come from?* "Make it bigger," Ellie commanded. But it faded back to only a glow.

Ellie peered through the hole. It was too small to crawl out. She knelt down and took a deep breath. *If I have special powers what can I do? Like Mom would say, "Move mountains." Yeah, really. Maybe the medal can regain its powers and do its magic again?* Maybe she had to give it a minute to recuperate. Then she heard a whistling sound. The light in the back flickered again. She heard the baron's voice.

"What do you have in your hand? Tell me or more rocks will come down."

To hear his voice again made Ellie tremble, but also angry. "You took this from Orly. Now it's mine, and it will help me."

"How can it? It's only metal. And it was mine because of the small turkey Orly brought me."

Can he really make more rocks fall? Ellie wondered. *But he's only a spirit. What power would he have?* She decided to ignore him. She stared at the medal. It still glowed. *Should I try again?* She aimed it at the corner of the hole. "Make it wider, please."

And again a beam shot out of the medal, and with a crack, more of the stones split off. "Thank you, thank you!" Ellie called out. She would have kissed the golden disc if it hadn't been so hot. She studied the opening. *Yes, it's wide enough.* She put the medal into her pocket and squeezed through the hole. She called back into the cave, "You didn't get your wish, Baron. I got out, but you never will."

She flopped down on the ground. *Where would he go anyway?* He was still as mean as before. Why should she care? She had to get home. Grandma probably had sent the police to search for her in the meantime.

Ellie straightened up and looked at the rocky outcrop above her. Now she had to climb up out of this gully. She couldn't see any other way around it. She placed some fallen rocks at the bottom to step on. But they were wobbly. She saw some straggly bushes on the slope she could hold onto and pull herself up. She took a deep breath and started.

At the beginning, she was slipping and sliding a lot. Sand and pebbles kept rolling away from under her fee. Finally, she got a hold of a branch of a bush and pulled herself higher. From then on the climbing got easier. Huffing and puffing, she made it to the top. She sat down and looked over the rim. "Quite a workout," her gym teacher would say.

Ellie felt proud of herself. She had met the baron, and he had told her where Orly was buried. The barn. But she couldn't remember a barn near Grandma's house. Like the old mansion it probably had been destroyed. Where would it have stood? Ellie could only hope that Grandma would remember hearing about it. Ellie smiled. Maybe Orly's medal would know. She took it out of her pocket. *This is the most awe-inspiring thing I have ever held in my hand. So much power in a metal disc. Does Orly know about it? I'll find out. Now I have to hurry. Can I find my way back?*

Chapter 10

Ellie stood for a moment and looked around. Everything was empty as if the whole village had disappeared. Oh no, she thought. Now I have to get the village back to find my way home. Suddenly, she felt tired. Would she be able to think hard enough to do it? Ellie closed her eyes. "Houses and people, come back."

She called it out twice. Then she noticed a faint outline of the street. At least she could follow it, even without buildings. She started jogging, afraid that it might disappear again.

All around, fog was rolling in, covering everything with a gray veil. Was it already night? What time could it be? Ellie looked at her watch but it had stopped. "The dumb battery again," she grumbled.

She tried to walk straight ahead. Where were the church and the big ovens? It could be that all the people were at home asleep. Ellie trotted on. Her insides were quivering.

Without houses, the whole area felt creepy, like being nowhere at all. Close by a small lake appeared. She hadn't seen that before. Did she go into the wrong direction? *I need to use my mind. Where am I?* Ellie closed her eyes again and thought hard. *I need to get home. Show me the proper way out.*

Nothing changed. Ellie knew that the baron was locked safely in the cave. He couldn't hurt anyone or cast a spell, could he? She walked toward the lake. But, just like in the cave, the closer she thought she got, the farther away it seemed to move. Maybe this time it was a sign not to go there. Ellie turned around. She didn't have time to waste.

The fog had lifted a bit, and she saw the church. "Oh boy, am I glad," she said out loud and marched quickly toward it.

The door opened, and people were coming out. Were these the same people Ellie had seen before? But that was such a long time ago. She heard a scream. A little boy pointed at her. "A ghost, there's a ghost!" He scrambled behind a woman and hid.

The woman patted his head and seemed to scold him. *He can see me. Grandma had told me that children see more than adults.* Ellie stood still and waited. Nobody else seemed to notice her.

The church goers drifted away, and Ellie heaved a sigh of relief. Like Orly had said, "Here you are a ghost, in your world, they are." She had never thought how complicated the world would be. At least now she could find her way home.

Then she heard a voice. "You cannot go home." There among trees Ellie saw something blue. Martha and her blue shawl. *What now?* Ellie had gotten the answer she had come for. Why couldn't she go back now?

She walked up to Martha. "Why can't I go home? The baron told me where Orly is."

Martha faded into just a shimmering outline then came back stronger. "You have to come with me," she said. With that, she turned and shuffled away.

Ellie knew she had to follow. There was a reason for Martha to ask her. Ellie sighed. Just when she thought she had come to the end of her adventure, things got in the way again. She tried to keep up with Martha's fast pace. Her figure was fading in and out, and Ellie didn't want to lose her.

After a few minutes, a small house appeared. *No bigger than Dad's toolshed*, Ellie thought. Martha waved at Ellie, turned, and disappeared inside. Ellie stepped through the door and waited. She could make out a table and two chairs. Faintly she noticed a fire in a small fireplace. Cozy warmth filled the room. Martha sat down on a bench near the window and pointed to a seat beside her.

How can I sit there? Ellie thought. *She isn't even real.*

But Martha started to talk. Even though her voice crackled and had an echo to it, Ellie could understand her. "You tried hard and did well," Martha said. "But you cannot go home now."

"Why not? I got my answer. I have to go back to my grandma. She will be worried and upset. I have been away for so long." *What else does she want me to do?*

Martha shook her head. "Time is everywhere and nowhere. It is yesterday, today, and tomorrow. Did you believe the baron?"

"Yes. He got angry because he had to tell me."

"He would be. What about his servants?" Martha became fainter.

Ellie worried that her whole figure would disappear. "They killed the baron. The baron said that Orly saw them stabbing him, so they killed Orly too."

Martha looked at her. "Do you believe that? Orly is still confused about who really killed the baron. You have to find it out."

"But how? The baron said, the servants did it. I can't do any more. Where would I go now and find out?" Ellie's insides were squirming and she was frustrated. *I really don't want to be here any longer.*

Martha got up. "You are tired and hungry. Take this." She put bread on the table. "It was baked this morning."

Ellie looked at it. *Real bread? Out of the big ovens?* She touched it. Yes, and it smelled good. "Thank you, but I still don't know—"

"I must go. I will leave you to take a rest. Use your mind." With that, the old lady walked to the end of the room and disappeared.

Chapter 11

Ellie sat for a while, looking at the spot from where Martha had disappeared. *Does she expect me to do miracles?* She turned back to the bread. What would two-hundred-year-old bread taste like? But she was hungry. She broke a piece off. Nice and soft inside and crusty outside. *This would have been even better with butter on it,* Ellie mused and took a big bite. *Hmm, good enough for a second piece.*

Ellie looked over to the fireplace. The flames were still spreading warmth. She took the chair and moved closer to the fire. *Why does Martha want me to stay here? What if I just took off?* She walked to the door and tried to open it. It was shut tight. She couldn't find a lock or a bolt. Through the small window she only saw darkness and fog. *Like being in a prison,* Ellie thought. She felt rebellion creeping up in her. All the work she had done and now Martha kept her locked up. What reason could she have? Ellie paced around. She didn't have the feeling that Martha disliked her. *Then why? What else am I supposed to figure out?*

"Make this house disappear and let me go home!" she called out.

However hard she thought about it, nothing happened. "Use your mind," Martha had said, again.

Well, I'm trying. I'm trying! But I'm tired. She walked over to the chair by the fire and plopped down. The warmth soothed her, and her eyes felt heavy. Ellie looked into the flames. They flickered and danced. Someone had told her once that she could see things in them if she concentrated.

Ellie pictured Orly. But she didn't see him. For a moment, she saw a hand and then something else. A knife.

Ellie jerked upright. Had she fallen asleep? She tried to focus her eyes. The fire had gone out. She looked around. The door was open, and Martha stood in the middle of the room.

"Can I go home now?" Ellie asked. *Please, please, let me go!*

"Did you sleep?" Martha asked. "Did you dream?"

Ellie shook her head. "I didn't dream. All I saw was a hand and a knife."

Again, she felt Martha looking through her.

"What kind of hand? Small or big? A man's or a child's?"

Ellie had to think. It had been just a flash—a blink of an eye, as Grandma would say. Ellie looked at her own hand. "It was big, not like mine," she said.

Martha seemed to smile. "You did well. Orlando will be happy. He did not kill the baron."

Ellie stared at her. "Of course not. He was knocked out. How could he have?" *What was Martha talking about?*

"Orlando will tell you. You can go now." Martha's voice grew soft again and the outline of her figure shimmered light blue. "Nurture your gift."

"Will I get better at it?" Ellie asked.

"Only if you want to," was Martha's answer.

Ellie felt sorry to see her go. Martha had been kind and helpful. But Ellie didn't understand her last remark about Orly not killing the baron. The baron had already blamed his servants for that.

All she could say was, "Thank you, Martha."

She stepped outside onto the now familiar dusty street with the houses all in a row and the people walking about. Ellie took a deep breath. Now she had to find her way through the forest. She touched the medal in her pants pocket. What a wonderful gift it had been. She was sure it would show her the way if she got lost.

As Ellie got into the forest, she smelled smoke. She looked back. Did it come from the chimneys of the houses or the big baking ovens? She couldn't see any. Ellie started to jog. Halfway through the trees, she saw flames. *Oh no! A wild fire? Where do I go now?* This was the only way to get home. She heard the crackling of the fire and felt the heat. Ellie looked back but the village was gone. *Do I have to run back deeper into the forest? I want to get home.* She yelled as loud as she could," Heeelp! I'm stuck here!"

Would anyone hear her?

Then a voice called, "Hey! What are you doing here? You have to get out—fast."

A fire fighter appeared through the smoke. Ellie ran to him. "I got lost, I didn't know. I have to get home."

The man shook his head. "Where were you? Didn't you hear the thunder? Lightning struck two trees and the fire started." As he pulled Ellie through the smoke, it started to rain. "Thank God," the fire fighter said. "That helps."

The rain drops are as big as grapes, Ellie thought. She didn't mind getting soaked—better than breathing in that smoke. She saw more men with water hoses and axes fighting the flames. As soon as Ellie stood on the safe side of the forest, the fire fighter looked at her.

"Are you sure you know where to go now? Do you live close by?"

"Yes, at the big house with my grandma. I like to explore the forest and I got lost." *Just a little white lie.*

The man nodded. "Good thing I heard you. Be more aware of your surroundings next time."

"Yes, thank you. I'd better run." Ellie didn't stop until she reached the end of the forest. She had never been so glad to see her beloved oak tree.

Chapter 12

Ellie leaned against the oak tree and stroked its bark. The air around her still smelled of smoke. But the rain had stopped. Why couldn't she have foreseen the fire? She had been so intent on getting home that she had forgotten everything else. Ellie sighed. To have the *gift* apparently meant more than only concentrating on something. She should have been listening for...what? Like the fire fighter said, everything around her. And maybe inside her?

Her heart pounded. What about Grandma? Could she be so worried she'd have a heart attack? After all she was old. Ellie ran over the field to where she expected the stone arch to be. But it wasn't there. Of course not. Orly wasn't either, not at this hour. She had to climb the fence to get into Grandma's garden. She stopped.

Grandma stood in the door as if she was waiting for her. "Well, at least you're home for supper," she called.

What? Supper? I must have been away for days. Here it seems to be only hours, Ellie thought. *Did the time really stand still?*

Grandma came toward her. "Where in heaven's name have you been?"

Ellie could see she was upset. Her voice was strong, but she didn't yell at Ellie.

"I was worried about the fire and you being in it," Grandma continued. "You look wet and bedraggled. Where exactly did you go?"

Ellie finally got her voice back. "All over the place. I found out everything about Orly."

"That will be quite a story." Grandma let out a sigh, touched Ellie's shoulder, and led her into the house. She looked at her again and took a deep breath. Then she shook her head. "I never thought I would have a grand-daughter with so much determination. Now go and have a shower. I'll look after supper."

Ellie took off her shoes and walked down the hall to the bathroom. Once she turned around and saw Grandma sitting at the table with her hands folded as if she was praying. Ellie felt bad. *Poor Grandma. She must have been in a panic.* Ellie had to make it up to her. But how? By telling her the whole story. That was only fair.

After the shower and washing her hair Ellie felt better. Would Grandma believe what Ellie had found out and how she did it? And now she had to find the place where the barn had been. Would Grandma still know anything about that?

Ellie made sure to take the medal out of her pants pocket before throwing the dirty clothes into the hamper. *I'll have to give it back to Orly.*

In the kitchen she slid onto her chair. She could hardly sit still in anticipation of telling about her adventure. Grandma ladled spaghetti and meatballs into bowls. How did she always know what Ellie liked? *I'll have to say something.* "I hope I didn't scare you too much. I forgot the time." *Another white lie.*

Grandma sat down. "After supper, you'll have to tell me." She looked at Ellie. "And don't leave anything out. It will be important. Right now, just eat."

After washing the dishes, Grandma walked into the living room and sat down on the sofa. "Start at the beginning," she said and patted the seat beside her.

Just like Martha, Ellie thought. She had to think of where to start. Yes, the first visit to the village. From there to finding the medal. She brought it out for Grandma to look at.

Grandma turned it over in her hand. "It must have been quite special for Orly."

"Yes, and I'll tell you later how it helped me. It's—it's miraculous." Ellie had to stop herself and keep on with her story. She continued about how Orly had told her about his death and that he still worried about it. Then the first time alone in the village.

Grandma didn't interrupt until Ellie told her about Martha.

She got up, went to a desk, and took a box out of a drawer. "My grandfather used to show me some pictures when I was a little girl. Some of them show his parents, aunts, and uncles, maybe even his grandparents." Grandma sorted through them. She took a big one out. "This must have been a family reunion. You can look at it. Who knows? Maybe Martha is in it. Grandpa told me that one of his aunts was a bit peculiar."

"Like being a seer? Why didn't they like her?" *That would have been so unfair.*

Grandma put the box aside. "Some people don't believe in it." She looked at Ellie. "That's why you have to be careful. You might have to keep it to yourself."

Ellie looked at the picture. She pointed to one woman. "That could be Martha. She's tall, just like I saw her. And she's wearing a shawl. It's really blue but here it shows only black and white." Then she remembered something. "Martha said that Orly was her sister's son. So he's Martha's nephew, isn't he?"

Grandma nodded. "And your cousin a few generations removed. That's why he was waiting for you all this time." She sat back with a far-away look on her face. "I was always told that, some times in the winter, a boy would show up in the fields. If they called out to him, he would disappear. So it wasn't a surprise to me that you met him. But tell me the rest of your story."

Ellie continued, relating how she went into the village, found the cave with the baron, the strange light and the falling rocks that closed the entrance. "You wouldn't believe what the medal did." Ellie explained how the beam cut a hole into the rocks and how she got out. She had to take a breath after that. She felt like she had done it all over again.

Grandma was quiet. Finally she said, "You're stronger than I thought, and inventive. Where did you learn that?"

"Dad always says, 'We have the brains and the tools to do it.'" Then Ellie told how Martha kept her in the house and made her fall asleep to be able see the knife and the hand. "All we have to find out is where the barn used to be. Do you remember anything about that?"

Grandma shook her head. "I have never seen a barn. My grandfather used the land for grazing cattle and for crops. But there must have been a barn of some sort. He needed room for tools and animals. His father could have built one." She picked up the box again. "Some pictures of the old house could be in here. Go ahead, look through them." She got up. "I have some work to do."

Ellie stood up too. "I'll take this up to my room if that's okay?"

Grandma nodded and Ellie climbed the stairs. *I have to take my time and look at every picture. But where would a barn have been? Next to the house or in the field? Will I ever be able to find the real Orly?*

Chapter 13

Ellie placed the box on her bed and sat next to it. So many pictures, some of them faded and brown. She needed to be patient and carefully study each one. That would take time. *Well, I have nothing else to do and this is a most important job.* At least she had come this far, and Orly was still waiting.

After half an hour, she hadn't seen a barn or similar building in any of the photos. Her eyes were tired, and she still had a full half box to go. In the meantime, it had turned dark outside, and Ellie switched on the lamp on her desk. There was a knock on her door. Grandma peeked in. "How are you doing, Ellie?"

"Not very successful. But I still have quite a few to go."

Grandma motioned downstairs. "Come for something to drink and some cookies. That might help."

Grandma always has the right ideas at the right time. Ellie followed her into the kitchen.

"You might need to look for an empty, big space near the house," Grandma suggested. "Maybe the barn was torn down at some point because it wasn't needed any more."

Ellie nodded. "That gives me an idea."

"And don't forget to go to bed," Grandma continued.

Ellie giggled. "I might fall asleep and dream about it."

After her snack, she continued turning over picture after picture until her head ached, and she couldn't suppress big yawns. *I'll look at the rest of the photos tomorrow,* she thought. *Somewhere I'll find something.* She took the medal out of her pocket. "Will you help me again?" she asked. "Maybe you still know where the barn used to be."

By now, her head was hurting more. Ellie went into the bathroom. *Maybe there are aspirins around.* But she needed to ask Grandma first.

"No wonder you have a headache," Grandma said and gave Ellie a pill and some water. "After a day like today, I would have one, too. Go to sleep right now. And call me if it gets worse."

Ellie still could not understand why she had been away for two days in the village and here only for some hours. If she had known, she wouldn't have worried so much about Grandma.

Lying in her bed, snuggled warmly under the comforter, Ellie thought that this was certainly better than on Martha's chair in front of the fire. Quickly she drifted off to sleep.

But her dreams were disturbing. One minute, she saw Martha motioning her to come, then the people coming out of the church, and finally she found herself in the cave again. It was cold and she shivered. When the cave filled with fire and she couldn't move, she let out a scream. When she opened her eyes, she saw Grandma standing by her bed.

"You had me worried, Ellie. What's the matter? Bad dreams?"

Ellie tried to sit up but her head was pounding, and she fell back onto the pillow.

Grandma felt her head and frowned. "Well, my child, you have a fever. You must have gotten a flu bug. I'll get you some hot lemon with honey and another pill."

"But I can't be sick. I have a job to do, and Orly is waiting." Ellie felt the familiar panic rising in her again.

"And soon Mom and Dad are coming back, and I'm still not ready." Tears were streaming down her face.

"Shush," Grandma said. "You'll make yourself sicker if you get upset. Rest up and you'll get well sooner. Besides, you can't do anything now. Wait until morning."

After the hot lemon drink and another aspirin, Ellie thought that Grandma was right—as always. After all, she had time until tomorrow. *As long as I get better fast. I have no time for this. That's what Mom would say.*

The sun's rays were streaming in between the curtains when Ellie woke up again. She kept still for a while and felt her head. Gingerly, she sat up. Okay, a bit better but there still was this spinning sensation.

A knock on the door announced Grandma. She came in with a tray in her hands. "How do you feel this morning?"

"I'm still a bit dizzy. Why is that?" Ellie tried to sit down on the edge of the bed.

Grandma put the tray down on the night table. "Don't expect to be totally all right so soon. I made a scrambled egg and toast for you." She looked at Ellie. "Is your stomach okay?"

Ellie nodded. "I think so. Thank you." Her stomach felt empty, and the food looked good. She ate some of it but couldn't finish it. *Maybe my stomach is still asleep. I don't want to waste time being sick.* She tried to stand up but had to close her eyes. *Is this how people feel when they're drunk? I'll never drink that stuff, ever.* She sat down again and finally crept back under the comforter. *Maybe another hour of sleep wouldn't hurt.*

Ellie woke up to a dark room. She sat up. Her head didn't spin anymore.

The door opened and Grandma looked in. "Are you feeling any better?"

"Yeah, but what time is it? It's already dark." *Impossible.*

Grandma switched on the bedside lamp. "You slept through the day. It's evening."

"Oh no. I wasted a whole day. You should have woken me up." Didn't Grandma know how important it was to get to Orly?

"Now, now." Grandma patted Ellie's head. "First, you have to get over this bug. Sleep was the best way to do it. Maybe you can look at more pictures. If you want, you can come downstairs for a nice cup of tea. Orly probably knows by now what's happened to you."

Oh, yeah, the pictures. Ellie still had a whole stack to look through. "All right, I'm coming down." She grabbed her sweater, put on socks, and carefully crept down the stairs. She didn't want to be dizzy again.

Chapter 14

After tea and a piece of toast with peanut butter, Ellie took the rest of the photographs out of the box. She turned each one over, searching for any sign of a barn. Grandma looked over her shoulder but didn't really help.

"You have better eyes than me," she said. "Besides, this is your quest. Just let me know if you notice anything interesting." She went to watch a TV show.

Ellie had almost come to the end of the pictures when she spotted one with three men standing in front of a building that did not look like a house. She could only see half of it: a big wooden door with two wooden beams crosswise over it. That was not a house door. It seemed heavy, old and worn.

"Grandma, come look. This could be a barn." *This has to be it!*

Grandma took the picture and held it under the light. "I don't remember seeing this building. But then I came here much later."

"But where could it have been? Close to the house or out in the field?" *Please, let it be nearby.*

"Where would you build a barn if you were a farmer with animals and hay to store?" Grandma asked.

Ellie thought for a moment. "Not too far away, but not next door. Animals smell, right? And hay has to be brought in from the field, so, fairly close to that." Then an idea came to her. "What if part of the barn was used to make this house bigger? Then it must have been right where your garden is now."

Grandma shook her head. "Maybe some of the wood could have been used for the house. But a barn was never right next to it."

Ellie's mood dropped. "Then we still don't know anything." She shuffled through some of the photos. She found two other ones with the same three men from the barn picture, this time they were sitting on a fence with a corner of the barn showing. *Where was this fence?* "Grandma, where would this fence have been?

At the end of your property where the stone arch stood?"

Grandma sighed. "Farmers fenced all their property in, all around. Let me see again." She held the photo under the lamp again and narrowed her eyes. "Tomorrow, we're going outside and take a close look, Ellie. Everything has changed so much." Then she chuckled. "We need an archaeologist to start a dig."

Ellie giggled, too. What if they would find hidden treasures? Tomorrow, yes. With a big yawn she packed up the pictures. "Good night, see you at breakfast," she said and climbed up the stairs.

Back in bed, she tried to go over the events after she had met Orly. But halfway through, her mind turned into blurry pictures with fences and old people waving at her.

∽∾∽

In the morning, Ellie couldn't wait to get outside and search for a likely spot where the barn could have been. "Do we have to eat breakfast, Grandma?" *What a waste of time.*

Grandma was already busy making French toast. "Nobody can work on an empty stomach, Eleanor. We have all day."

"Yes, but Orly—"

"He's waited this long, he can wait a little longer."

Of course, Grandma was right, again. And the French toast was delicious.

When the breakfast dishes were finally done, Ellie grabbed the two pictures she had selected and checked them once more. She heard Martha's voice, "Use your mind." Ellie concentrated on the three men sitting on the fence. Faintly an image appeared. Ellie blinked. The stone arch.

Without waiting, Ellie raced down the steps into the garden. She ran to where the stone arch had been. Right next to it stood the fence in the same place as the old one once had. She looked closely at the photo again. There at the end showed the corner of the barn. It must have stood where the lawn now grew with two poles and Grandma's clothes line on it. This had to be it.

"Grandma, come look," Ellie called. "I think I've found the place for the barn."

Grandma shaded her eyes against the sun. "Why are you so sure?"

Ellie showed her the picture. "The stone arch appeared here." She pointed to the spot she saw on the photo. "Right next to it is the corner of the barn. It's now under the grass."

"And how do you figure we can find out for sure? I'm not having my lawn dug up."

Ellie knew that Grandma was not happy. She

sighed. "I can tell Orly where he is, but we can't dig him up?"

Grandma shook her head. "We would have to excavate everything. It has been there for two-hundred years, Ellie. Heaven knows what else was built on top before our house."

Ellie took a deep breath. "I've seen a show where people go over the ground with a machine to find treasure or things they want to dig up. Do you know someone with something like that?"

Grandma stared at her. "Do you think that machine could register a skeleton? I don't know about that. Metal, maybe, but bones? Besides, I don't know anyone in the city who could do it."

Ellie's heart sank. Digging up a skeleton was creepy enough, but what was she going to tell Orly? Would it be enough for him to know where he was buried? Of course, he would be happy that he didn't kill the baron. Ellie still couldn't figure out why he thought he did. "I'll talk to Orly as soon as possible. He has to know everything I've found out."

Grandma walked back to the house. She turned and looked at Ellie. "Will you promise me not to disappear again, Eleanor?"

"Yes, Grandma, I promise. I'll just go looking for Orly and be back for lunch."

Grandma nodded. "It's early yet. You might as well go."

Ellie jogged back through the garden toward the fence. She stopped. Where was the stone arch? She stood and waited. She visualized the arch. *Come on, come back. I need to find Orly.* Nothing happened. Had Orly given up on her? But he needed the information Ellie had found for him. Was he already in the village? Ellie sat down on the bench. *Everybody tells me to have patience. But I don't have any. It's too hard.*

Chapter 15

Ellie sat on the bench and tried to calm down. But her mind flip-flopped on what to tell Orly first: the church and Martha or the cave. No, it had to be told from the beginning. After all, Orly had to realize all the work she had done for him. That was only fair. Hopefully, he would show up again.

There! The stone arch! Ellie had been so deep in thought that she hadn't seen it right away. She jumped up and ran through it. From farther away Orly's flute song floated towards her. Ellie called, "Where are you? I've been waiting." The sound of the flute came nearer. Finally, she saw Orly standing by his favorite tree. She let out a breath of relief. "I have so much to tell you."

Orly stuck the flute into his pants pocket. "I thought you didn't make it back. Then your Grandma said that you were sick."

Ellie's eyes popped open. "My grandma? How?"

"I picked up her thoughts. They are very strong. What can you tell me? Was it dangerous?"

Ellie sat down on a tree stump. "It's a long story, but with a good ending." She pulled the medal out of her pants pocket. "This is amazing. It helped me to get—but I'll tell you from the beginning." She started the story with her way into the forest.

Orly listened quietly. Once in a while, he smiled or nodded. He could barely sit still when Ellie's story came to the cave with the baron. He took the medal and turned it over and over. "It has never melted anything for me. It was just a keepsake from my grandfather. Maybe he knew about it." He gave it back to Ellie.

"But it's yours," she protested. "I can't keep it."

Orly's face was serious. "Maybe it can show you where I am, if you ask it."

"Yes, I thought about that too. I think I know now where the barn used to be and where they buried you. But—" *How am I going to tell him?*

"But what?"

Ellie took a deep breath. "The barn stood where Grandma's garden and lawn are now. And she doesn't want to dig big holes all over. It would mess everything up." She looked into Orly's eyes and saw disappointment.

But, after a pause, he sat up straight. "At least I know where I am and that I didn't kill the baron."

Yes, the big question. "I've always wondered why you thought you killed him. You were knocked out and couldn't have done it."

"But I came to and the baron was lying dead beside me, and the knife was bloody."

Ellie started to understand. "Then the servants must have come back and stabbed you too."

Orly shook his head. "I do not remember. They must have hated the baron a lot. But why me?"

"Because they thought you had seen them killing him. They didn't want you as a witness."

Orly got up and looked at Ellie. "You have been so brave." But his eyes got serious again. "What am I going to do if I cannot get buried in the village? I'll still have to stay between your world and mine."

Ellie's heart sank. "You mean you have to be re-buried? But how? You can't carry..." She didn't know what to think.

Orly shuffled his feet. "At least I'll need to have a part of myself."

"So you mean a part of your bones?"

Orly nodded. "Those are the rules."

Ellie felt a bit better. "Oh, good. I couldn't see anyone carrying a whole skeleton through the forest. First, we still have to find the exact spot where you are. Even then, Grandma won't allow everything to be dug up." She thought for a moment. "You know what? I'll ask your medal. Maybe it still remembers, and then we'll know for sure."

Orly's face lit up. He took the disc out of Ellie's hand and stroked it. "Tell me where I am," he whispered. "I need to know." Again he gave it back to Ellie. "Please, try. I'll meet you again tomorrow." He pulled out his flute, but before he started to play he said, "I want to thank you for going through all the dangers, but I do not know how."

"We'll talk about that later. First things first, like my Mom always says. See you tomorrow." She stood up and walked toward the stone arch. She waved at Orly, and he started to play.

Since it was almost lunchtime, Ellie thought it better to go right back to the house. She couldn't let Grandma wait again. And she would help her wash the dishes. Maybe then Grandma would let her dig at least a small part in the garden? Orly's medal was her last hope. Wasn't that the reason why she had found it in the forest? *It might just all fit together*, Ellie thought.

Chapter 16

Grandma had set the table when Ellie arrived. "You kept your promise," Grandma said. "Did you see Orly?"

Ellie nodded. "I told him my whole story—" She stopped.

Grandma leaned her hands on the table. "And?"

"We still have a problem. We just *have* to find his skeleton. He needs at least one bone to get back to his village. Or else he has to stay where he is. And that would be just too awful. And all my work would have been for nothing." She grabbed her fork and stirred around in the noodles on her plate.

Grandma sat down. "Any plans how to do that?"

"I'll have to really think about that. I'll have to use my mind, like Martha told me to." Ellie looked up at Grandma. "Remember? I did manage to see the stone arch on the photo. Maybe I can see something in the ground." She thoughtfully chewed her food. After she swallowed it, she continued, "I also have his medal. The medal was around when Orly was killed. I'll bet it knows where he is."

Grandma sighed. "Let nobody tell me that life is easy. This last week has been…"

"Too difficult?" Ellie got worried. *What if Grandma never invites me again?*

Grandma took a sip out of her teacup. "Well, I would call it eye opening." Then she frowned. "As I said before, no bulldozer is digging up my garden. I hope you can find another way. I don't want Orly to stick around forever either. I feel for him." She got up. "I have my ladies coming in again today. I'll better get busy."

Ellie swallowed. *Oh no. Do I have to drink tea with them again?* "Grandma, I don't have to be around for that, right? They've already met me."

"Why not, Ellie?"

"I get embarrassed when they all look at me."

"Whatever for?"

"Too many eyes?" Ellie mumbled. "And I'll be very busy."

Grandma chuckled. "Get on then. Do your job. I'll keep my fingers crossed."

As promised, Ellie did the lunch dishes and even dried them. She still hoped that this would get Grandma into a good mood. What if she only had to dig up a few shovels full of grass? It would grow back quickly, wouldn't it? She heard the ladies' voices outside and scooted out the back door.

Again, Ellie sat down on the bench in the garden and closed her eyes. She tried hard to think of nothing but the place where the barn once stood. She envisioned it as much as she knew from the picture and pretended to walk into the building. Would it have been full of hay and straw, maybe with even an animal or two? Two hundred years ago, it couldn't have been empty. In the winter, the baron would have stored everything in it.

Ellie opened her eyes. She hadn't seen anything like a hole in the floor. This was going to be hard, maybe impossible. *I'm just not a good enough seer yet.*

She took Orly's medal out of her pants pocket and turned it over in her hand. "You're Orly's and my only hope," she told it. "You know that, right? Please, don't let us down." She walked over to the fence that had bordered the barn so many years ago. Then she turned right and stepped onto the lawn with the wash line poles. Step by step, she paced it off, holding the medal and aiming it at the ground. It did not react. Once in a while, Ellie thought that it got warmer, but nothing like before in the cave.

When Ellie had walked over the whole grassy area without even a quiver from the medal, her hopeful mood dropped. *Now what? How can I use my mind better? What would Martha do?* She looked up at the oak tree. Well, Martha wouldn't be able to climb up there but Ellie could. She had done it before, and it felt really nice sitting on the branch. Maybe some ideas would come to her up in among the rustling leaves.

As Ellie sat on her favorite branch, she wondered if she could see a sign down on the grass. Sometimes looking at it from above could make a difference. What if she tried to imagine the barn on top of the lawn? And then what? She couldn't get inside and dig. Why didn't the medal help as it did in the cave? *Wait a minute! It was pitch-dark in the cave, not in the sunshine like now. Can it be that it only works at night?* Ellie's mind raced. How could she make that happen? She would have to get up in the middle of the night and try again. Without waking Grandma. That would need planning.

Chapter 17

Ellie heard the voices of Grandma's ladies and knew they were leaving. It was safe to climb down from her branch. She looked once more over at the field. Again, she wondered: were was Orly when she didn't see him? Did he make himself visible only when he wanted to talk to her? And in the meantime? Ellie would probably never find out. Maybe she should try and ask him tomorrow. But now she had to plan her next step: how to sneak out of the house in the middle of the night. She could only hope that Grandma was a deep sleeper.

Ellie looked again at the medal. "All my hope is on you. You must have seen where the servants buried Orly. You helped me once, now you have to help him. His grandfather would have wanted you to." She sighed. *I'm talking to a medal, only a shiny thing. But, to me, it's more than that, it's alive. I hope it listens.*

When Ellie opened the screen door, she saw that Grandma was already busy making supper. "Two more days and your parents will be back," she said.

Ellie stopped. "What? Already? But I'm not done yet."

Grandma looked at her. "You'll have to dream up something. You've come this far, don't give up. Did you find anything?"

Ellie shook her head. "No, but I think I will try one more thing." *Sorry, I can't tell you the rest.*

Grandma turned the pork chops over in the frying pan. "I still cannot believe what you did during your visit. You've made some big discoveries. They'll be with you for the rest of your life."

"I don't think I'll find any more Orlys and villages like his." Ellie thought for a moment. "But I'll miss him and Martha too. They're special. It would be nice if they could come around sometime." Ellie put plates on the table. "At what time does it get dark, Grandma?"

"Around nine or close to ten o'clock. Why?"

"Part of my idea. It's a secret."

Grandma furrowed her brow. "Don't play tricks on me, Eleanore. I go to bed at ten, you know that. And I want you in bed too."

"It's nothing bad, I promise. Just some…research." *Was that the right word?*

"Whatever it is, I want to deliver you in one piece to your parents."

Ellie laughed. "Don't worry so much, Grandma, I'm a big girl."

"Oh, sure. Go and eat your green beans."

After supper, Ellie dug out her diary again to pass the time. There was so much she wanted to write since her last try. She sat on the rocker on the porch with a big cushion on her lap, placed the diary on top, and started.

The village.

She had gotten as far as the cave with the baron when she heard Grandma's voice.

"Come in and have some brownies and lemonade."

"With chocolate icing?" Ellie called back.

"That's for you to find out," came the answer.

Ellie closed her diary. She had lots of time to finish later. Brownies were important. Then she had to wait until Grandma went to bed so she could sneak outside. It had to work. What else could she do?

After Ellie ate a big square of brownies and licked the chocolate icing from her fingers, she couldn't think of anything else to do. Grandma had to be asleep before she could try out Orly's medal. "Is it okay if I take a shower before going to bed, Grandma?"

Grandma was deeply involved in a detective show on TV. But she turned around. "Go ahead, Ellie. If you need anything, let me know."

After the shower, Ellie got into her pajamas. *I'll just put my pants overtop when I go out later*, she thought. She yawned. *I'll take a little nap. When I wake up, Grandma will be fast asleep.*

Someone calling her name woke Ellie out of a deep sleep. She sat up. Everything was dark and quiet. Who was calling? How late was it? Ellie jumped up and grabbed her pants. The little clock on the table showed two o'clock. *Oh, no! I've overslept. Is it too late? Was that Orly calling to wake me up?*

Ellie opened her bedroom door as softly as she could. She listened at Grandma's door. She could hear a soft snore. *Good, now down the stairs.* Ellie had to be careful to miss the second last step because it squeaked. She grabbed a flashlight from the hall table and tiptoed to the back door. It was easier to open than the front one. Outside, she stood still for a moment and listened. How different the garden felt from the daytime. All the colors had turned gray and black. The wind made shooshing noises through the trees. Everything else around her seemed to be asleep.

Carefully, Ellie plodded her way through the garden toward the grassy part. She touched Orly's medal in her pants pocket. It was still cold. She took it out and shone the flashlight on it. "Will you help me one more time?" she whispered.

With the medal pointing downward, Ellie started to walk from the left side of the lawn up to the end, then turning and going back again. Her stomach had a knot in it. What if Orly wasn't buried here at all? What if the baron had lied? "Trust your instincts," Martha had said.

After walking up and down three times, the medal in her hand felt warm. Toward the middle of the fourth row, it got so hot that Ellie could only hold it between her thumb and forefinger. Her heart pounded. "Show me! Show me!" she pleaded, trying to keep her voice down.

The flashlight showed something in the ground moving. A strip of grass opened up as if the medal had sliced right through it. Ellie stopped and moved the golden disc up and down the furrow. It got deeper and wider. She held her breath. What was really down there?

She aimed the flashlight into the hole. It revealed something looking like tattered cloth with small yellow pieces sticking out of it. Ellie got on her knees, pointed the flashlight again, and looked closer. Then she gasped and sat back on the grass."Oooh!" A skull had stared at her. She had to swallow a few times. *Why do skulls have to look so scary? It's just bones.* But she couldn't help shuddering. *I can't take it out. No way. I need a long stick to find something else.* She got up and shone the light around. There by the wash line pole stood something shiny. She ran toward it: Grandma's mini rake for the flower beds. That would do.

Ellie knelt again by the hole and carefully moved some of the dark pieces aside. "I have to do this. I have to do this," she told herself and tried not to look at the skull. She let out another gasp. The yellow pieces sticking out were bones too, all parts of Orly.

Quietly she called out, "Orly, is this you? I need to know."

Did he even hear her? She knew he was not able to come over to her side. How could he help her? Ellie listened. Was it the wind or a voice whispering? No, she heard a soft whistle like a flute—Orly's flute.

That had to be his way to answer her question. But what now? How to retrieve a bone for him? *I can't possibly touch one of those. And which one? Down there is his whole skeleton.*

Gently, Ellie probed a bit more around in the hole. Some pieces came away and revealed a hand: five fingers. Ellie had seen a skeleton in the Science Center. How neat and clean that had been. Orly had lain here for so long, everything had rotted away, except his bones and bits and pieces of his clothing.

How to get the hand out of there? There is no way I can touch it.

Then she heard a voice in her head. '*Why not? You touched Orly's hand even when he was a ghost to you. It's the same person.* That could only be Martha's voice.

Ellie knelt again. She positioned the rake over the hand and tried to hook it underneath. But as she tried to lift it, the hand broke apart. "Oh, bummer," Ellie grumbled. *What now? Do I have to pick up every finger? I want Orly to have his whole hand.* She took a breath and, with the help of the little rake, managed to retrieve two fingers, then one more, the palm of the hand, and finally the last two fingers. "Whew!"

Carefully, Ellie dropped the pieces onto the grass and reassembled them. To her surprise the parts slowly fitted together into one hand. She glanced at the still glowing medal. "Did you do that? You're amazing." It was a small hand, like her own. Not the big one she saw in Martha's fire place.

What about the rest of Orly? This was his grave. It had to be marked. At home people would put plaques with names on them. She was going to do the same here. It was only right.

Chapter 18

Ellie needed something to wrap up the hand. Maybe an old towel or some paper. She shone the flashlight around but it was too dark to find anything. She remembered a few pieces of cloths on the porch by the flower pots to mop up spilled water.

With her flashlight lighting the path, Ellie sprinted to the house. She found two small rags and ran back to the grave. With one rag around her own hand, she carefully picked up Orly's bones and placed them on the other cloth. She looked at the grave. To her surprise the big hole in the grass started to close up.

"Wait a minute!" she called out. "I need to remember the exact spot so I can put a proper marker on it."

She placed the little rake lengthwise over the faint line in the grass. Then the line disappeared too.

Ellie picked up the medal. "Thank you for all your help. You even closed up the hole. How do you do that? Tomorrow you can go back to Orly." With his hand securely wrapped in the rags, Ellie walked back to the house. Inside, everything was quiet. *I hope Grandma didn't wake up to check on me. Then I'm in trouble.* But she had to smile. *I did it. I rescued Orly.*

Quietly, she climbed up the stairs and opened her bedroom door.

Now she felt tired. Her bed looked so inviting. She placed the hand on the desk, stripped off her shoes and pants, and flopped down on the bed. Later, she wondered why she hadn't taken off her socks.

The next thing Ellie heard was Grandma calling. "You're a sleepyhead today. Breakfast is waiting."

Ellie threw the covers off and zipped into the bathroom. "I'm coming!" *I've overslept again. Orly must be waiting.*

Grandma smiled when Ellie sat down at the table. "How did your adventure turn out last night?"

Ellie's mouth fell open. How did she know? "What—what adventure?"

Grandma chuckled. "You didn't think I wouldn't check up on you during the night, did you? As long as I could see you and the light outside, I wasn't too worried. I knew you were looking for Orly's grave. What did you find?"

Ellie had to swallow a few times. "I thought you would be mad at me for skipping out in the middle of the night and call me back."

"What good would that have done? You had to bring it to the end."

Thoughtfully, Ellie peeled her boiled egg. "Thank you, Grandma. Yes, I found his grave. I'll have to show you where it is and what I dug out. And your lawn is back to normal." Between scooping out the egg and buttering her toast she told Grandma the story of Orly's hand.

Grandma didn't say much, just shook her head and poured herself another cup of tea.

"Orly probably waits already," Ellie said. "Maybe he even saw me out there last night. I think I heard his flute."

"Then you cannot wait too long. Your parents are coming this afternoon. Now show me the hand."

Ellie looked at Grandma. "Are you sure? It's not very nice looking. It was pretty icky down in the grave."

"I promise I won't faint," Grandma assured her.

Ellie brought the hand down from her bedroom, placed it on the table, and unfolded the cloth. "See, only bones."

Grandma took a look. "Poor Orly. A two-hundred-year-old little hand. You better take it to him. Now he won't have to come by in the winter anymore."

Ellie didn't wait any longer. She walked slowly down the porch steps to keep the parcel safe. At the end of the garden, the stone arch appeared. She could hear the soft melody of the flute. She stopped for a second. *I will never hear it again or see Orly after today. S*adness made her throat feel tight. *I might never see the stone arch either.* A tear rolled down her cheek as she stepped through the arch.

Orly sat on his favorite tree stump and played the flute. When he saw Ellie, he stopped in mid-tune and got up. As Ellie stood in front of him, she suddenly didn't know what to say. She just unfolded the rags and held the hand out to him.

Orly touched each finger gently and nodded. "Yes, it's mine. I feel it wants to be with me." He looked at Ellie. "I heard you yesterday night. I have nothing I can thank you with. You have been the best friend I've ever had."

"I'm really sorry I can't see you and talk to you anymore. I'll miss you," Ellie said. "But don't worry about a present or anything. I had a super-duper adventure." She had to giggle. "That baron was a miserable guy. I wonder how long he has to stay in the cave."

Orly was still looking at his hand. "You were so brave. And I can go home now."

Ellie took the medal out of her pocket and handed it to him. But he shook his head.

"*That* is my present to you. You keep it and think of me." Ellie tried to protest, but Orly insisted. "You will have better use for it than I since you are like Martha." He turned. "You want to go with me to the forest?"

Together they walked toward the big oak tree. "What will the village people say when you arrive?" Ellie asked. "Will they even remember you?"

Orly smiled. "They have waited a long time because they could never find me. And Martha will be happy."

"I want you to say hello to her from me. She helped me a lot."

Orly tucked his flute into his pant pocket. "Martha will be happy that you remember her."

As they walked past the oak tree, Ellie thought the edge of the forest came up too quickly. Orly turned and stretched out his hand. Ellie grabbed it. *It feels so real.* "Good bye, Orly."

He nodded. "Have a good life, Ellie." He stepped into the forest, turned once, and waved. Then the outlines of his figure dimmed and disappeared.

"Bye, Orly," Ellie whispered again. She went back to the oak tree and wrapped her arms around it. Her insides felt empty. *Every time I come here, I'll probably be looking for Orly.* Two tears slipped down her cheeks. She brushed them away and straightened up. She still had one more thing to do. Somewhere in Grandma's shed had to be a piece of wood she could use as a marker for Orly's grave. She would carve his name on it and place it on the site. *That will have to do for now until I find something better.*

Ellie wandered back over the meadow through the arch. As she turned back, it faded away. She sat down on the bench and turned the medal over in her hand. *This will be my guide, my very best friend with a little bit of Orly in it.* Would Mom and Dad believe what she had done and why? Would they believe that she was able to see and hear things they couldn't? Then Ellie smiled. *I have the best witnesses in the world: the medal and Grandma!*

THE END

About the Author

Gisela Woldenga was born in Oldenburg, Germany, on July 21, 1934. As soon as she could read, she started to write: little poems and fairy tales. She still has some of them. When she finished high school, she started working in a lawyer's office, mostly disputes over last wills and testaments and property. Then she moved on to the main taxation office. She met her husband through pen-paling—he was already in Canada—and she joined him in 1954 in Ontario. She had her first baby in 1956, her second one in 1957, then moved to Vancouver BC and added another baby in 1961.

Woldenga picked up music (piano) again in 1964, started teaching shortly after, and taught until about six years ago. In the meantime, she wrote articles, poems, children's stories. She also took up acting after her kids were safely gone, in 1998. Lots of fun! She's still doing it whenever possible. After some courses in writing for children, she started publishing. From there on into short stories for adults and, finally, six books.